# A Note to Parents and Teachers

The *Dorling Kindersley Readers* series is a reading programme for children, which is highly respected by teachers and educators around the world. The LEGO Company has a global reputation for offering high quality, innovative products, specially designed to stimulate a child's creativity and development through play.

Now Dorling Kindersley has joined forces with The LEGO Company, to produce the first-ever graded reading scheme to be based around LEGO play themes. Each *Dorling Kindersley Reader* is guaranteed to capture a child's imagination, while developing his or her reading skills, general knowledge and love of reading.

The books are written and designed in conjunction with literacy experts, including Cliff Moon M.Ed., Honorary Fellow of the University of Reading.

Cliff Moon spent many years as a teacher and teacher educator, specializing in reading. He has written more than 140 books for children and teachers, and he reviews regularly for teachers' journals.

The four levels of *Dorling Kindersley Readers* are aimed at different reading abilities, enabling you to choose the books that are right for each child.

**Level 1** – Beginning to Read
**Level 2** – Beginning to Read Alone
**Level 3** – Reading Alone
**Level 4** – Proficient Readers

The "normal" age at which a child begins to read can be anywhere from three to eight years old, so these levels are only guidelines.

**Dorling Kindersley**
LONDON, NEW YORK, SYDNEY, DELHI, PARIS,
MUNICH and JOHANNESBURG

**Senior Editor** Cynthia O'Neill
**Senior Art Editor** Nick Avery
**Senior Managing Editor**
Karen Dolan
**Managing Art Editor**
Cathy Tincknell
**DTP Designer** Jill Bunyan
**Production** Chris Avgherinos
**Picture Researcher** Andrea Sadler

**Reading Consultant**
Cliff Moon M.Ed.

First published in Great Britain in 2000 by
Dorling Kindersley Limited
9 Henrietta Street
London WC2E 8PS

2 4 6 8 10 9 7 5 3 1

A CIP catalogue record for this book is
available from the British Library.

ISBN 0-7513-7259-5

Colour reproduction by Dot Gradations, UK
Printed and bound by L Rex, China

The publisher would like to thank the following for their
kind permission to reproduce their photographs:
c=centre; b=bottom; l=left; r=right; t=top

Mary Evans Picture Library: Endpapers 26cra;
Robert Harding Picture Library: 39tr;
Science Photo Library: 26tl; Pekka Parviainen 5br; Simon Fraser 11tr;
Telegraph Colour Library: 31tr; Hubert Manfred 21tr; V.C.L 8br;
Topham Picturepoint: 25tr.

For our complete
catalogue visit
**www.dk.com**

# Contents

DK DORLING KINDERSLEY *READERS* **LEGO**

# *MISSION* TO THE *ARCTIC*

Written by Nicola Baxter • Illustrated by Roger Harris

READING **3** ALONE

DK

A Dorling Kindersley Book

# Meteor alert!

"Captain Ross? I need your help!"

At the LEGO Space Port Centre, a scientist named Cosmo was making an urgent call.

"I've had great news!" Cosmo went on. "A massive meteor shower has just entered Earth's atmosphere! According to our readings, the meteorites didn't burn up. Many of them have landed – in the Arctic Circle.

I need to send a team to the Arctic at once. Will you lead it for me?"

**Meteors**

A meteor is a piece of space dust or rock, which burns up if it enters the Earth's atmosphere, leaving a bright trail. Meteors can occur on their own, or in showers.

Two days later, at a secret location near the Arctic, Captain Ross addressed a team of explorers and scientists.

"Welcome to Mission Meteorite," he said, smiling.

Everyone in the room was vital to the success of the mission.

Doc was the medical expert. Crystal had grown up in the Arctic and knew how to survive the harsh conditions. Scooter, a researcher and mechanic, would keep the team's vehicles going. Finally, there was Cosmo, the geologist who had asked that the team be set up.

"We'll set up a base tomorrow," said the captain. "Wherever those meteorites landed, we'll find them."

The next day, an icebreaker edged through the ice sheet covering the Arctic Ocean. The engines roared. Crushed ice screeched against its hull. In the ship's hold was special equipment needed for Mission Meteorite.

*The Arctic is the most northern part of the Earth. It is covered with snow and ice all year round.*

Captain Ross and his team were headed to an icy wasteland. Special LEGO vehicles were essential – the team had to be prepared for any problem.

The captain chose a place to dock, unload the ship and set up the Polar Base. Once the work was finished, it was time to explore.

Space Port satellites had found four places where the meteorites might have landed. Most of the team members were heading in different directions, to search the area. Doc would guard the base.

Although it was cold, the sun was shining brightly. The team wore goggles to protect their eyes from the glare.

"Check your watches!" called Captain Ross.

### Midnight Sun

The Sun hardly rises at the North Pole for six months a year. For the rest of the year, it barely sets, shining at midnight!

"Remember, this is one of the most dangerous places on Earth. Contact each other every 30 minutes."

Scooter headed north, driving the sturdy Polar Scout. The skis hissed as he sped over the snow and ice.

Scooter had been travelling for around 15 minutes, when all at once he heard a loud whistling above his head. He looked up.

Glowing lights were streaking across the sky. More meteorites were bombarding the Arctic!

Scooter was so stunned by what he had seen that he didn't notice a bank of snow ahead. The Scout hit the slope and lurched to the left. Scooter was thrown through the air.

# Scooter in danger

Scooter was not badly hurt but, unluckily, the Scout was damaged. One ski was badly twisted.

It would take Scooter a long time to fix the Scout. He had the tools he needed but he was wearing thick gloves which would slow him down. Still, it was too dangerous to take them off.

"Doc warned me about frostbite," Scooter muttered, as he opened the toolbox. He knew that frozen body parts soon turn black and have to be amputated. Many explorers have lost toes or fingers in that way.

Scooter concentrated hard on mending the twisted ski. He didn't notice the shadow looming over him until it was too late...

### Arctic clothing

Arctic explorers wear insulated clothing, to keep warm in below-freezing temperatures, and goggles, to protect their eyes.

As the polar bear looked down at him, Scooter was too afraid to move. The bear was so close that Scooter could hear its breathing. He did not dare reach for his radio to call for help. He had never felt so alone.

The massive bear could kill Scooter with just one blow from its paw. Poor Scooter trembled as he looked up into the bear's black eyes. The horrible silence seemed to go on forever.

Then a cry broke the stillness.

**Polar bears**

Polar bears only live in the Arctic. They are the biggest hunters in the area, and can swim, dive and climb trees as well!

A vivid red flare shot across the sky as Crystal whizzed over the ice on her Snow Scooter. The polar bear ran off.

"She must have cubs nearby," said Crystal, as she drew up to Scooter. "She was trying to protect them."

"Lucky you came along," he panted. "Not luck," said Crystal. "We knew something was wrong when you didn't make radio contact after 30 minutes. Let's go, Scooter. The captain has called everyone back to base."

# A crack in the ice

Several miles away, Captain Ross had turned his Ice Surfer to head for base. Freezing winds tugged at the sail as he 'surfed' the snow.

*A permanent sheet of ice floats on the surface of the Arctic Ocean. Sometimes ice breaks off this sheet. It floats on the open water below and is called pack ice.*

Suddenly, he heard a creaking and groaning. It seemed to come from the ice all around him.

To his horror, Captain Ross saw a vast crack appear in the ice before him and the ground open up. The captain tried to slow down, but there was not enough time to stop...

As the captain fell into the crevasse, he flung out his arms. Years of mountaineering had made his fingers strong. He clawed at a narrow ledge and struggled to find a foothold.

His Ice Surfer dangled on the cliff edge. The icy ocean churned below.

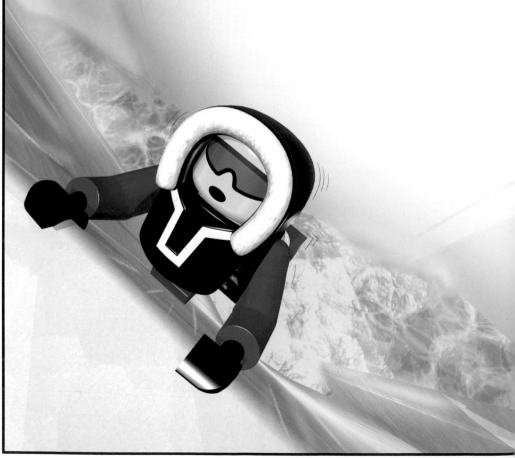

The captain had to save himself,
and his vehicle. Without it, he could
never make it back to base.

Captain Ross hauled himself up
slowly. He was careful not to look down
at the freezing waters.

By the time he reached the top,
he was exhausted. He barely had the
strength to pull the Ice Surfer to safety.

Captain Ross smiled shakily. The difficult job was done. He had made it to safety.

Picking up his radio from the Ice Surfer, he made contact at once with the base camp.

"Captain Ross! Where are you?" said Crystal. She sounded very anxious. "What's happened?"

"I'll explain back at base," panted the captain. "Tell the team not to worry."

He climbed onto his Ice Surfer and set off back to camp.

But at the Polar Base, bad news was waiting for him.

Cosmo was missing.

## Dog power

Early Arctic explorers travelled on wooden sledges, pulled by a team of dogs. The dogs are called huskies.

*The first explorer to reach the North Pole was the American, Robert Peary, in 1909.*

*Sometimes meteorites are massive. This crater in Arizona, USA, was caused thousands of years ago when a meteorite hit Earth.*

Cosmo had not made radio contact with the base. Everyone was worried about him, but they tried not to panic and kept busy. Scooter made notes about the meteor shower he had seen. Crystal recorded facts about the weather conditions.

Doc gave Captain Ross a check-up.

"You've been lucky," he said.
"Nothing but scrapes and bruises."

"They're the least of my worries..."
the captain began. A blast of cold air
stopped him as the door was flung open.

"Captain!" cried Cosmo. "I've found
a meteorite!"

# Mystery of the meteorite

Cosmo told his incredible story.

"There's been a new meteorite shower..." he began.

"I saw it, too!" Scooter broke in.

"One landed quite near to me, so I reached it in minutes. But it was very strange," Cosmo told them.

"There was a light in the sky, like the Northern Lights. And I thought I heard a *humming* noise," he finished.

"Why didn't you contact us?" asked Captain Ross.

"I ran away," Cosmo said, blushing. "And I dropped my radio as I ran. It was too weird on my own."

Early the next morning, the
Caterpillar Outpost set off to search
for the meteorite. Inside was all the
equipment the team needed. There was
even a portable laboratory.

Cosmo and Crystal were in the Cat.
Captain Ross flew the helicopter with
Doc, watching out for cracks in the ice.
Scooter stayed behind at camp.

**Helicopters**

Unlike aeroplanes, helicopters do not need long runways to take off or land. This makes them ideal for journeys in places such as the Arctic.

"It looks like Cosmo has reached his marker flag," said Doc at last. "Hey! That rock is glowing!"

When the team gathered near to
the meteorite, Doc was not the only one
to look surprised.

"Wow!" gasped Crystal.

From a distance, the meteorite
seemed to glow with a strange blue light.

"My instruments show nothing,"
said Captain Ross. "No magnetic field.
No electrical field. Nothing."

Cosmo took a deep breath and walked up to the meteorite.

"What can you see?" cried Crystal.

"Make your report," ordered the captain.

"You won't believe this..." Cosmo began.

*Up to half a tonne of meteorites land on Earth each year. Over a dozen have been found that come from the planet Mars.*

### Extraterrestrial life

All the living things that we know live on our planet. So far, no one has proved that there is life anywhere else in the universe.

Cosmo was right. For a moment, no one believed him.

"A fossil from space? Pull the other one!" laughed Doc, as the team walked towards Cosmo.

"That would be news!" said Crystal.

But seconds later, they saw Cosmo was telling the truth. The team stared in amazement at the glowing fossil.

"Does this mean what I think it means?" asked the captain, at last. "Is it proof of life on other planets?"

"No," sighed Cosmo. "This fossil must be millions of years old. But it's certainly proof that there *was* life on other planets!"

"I can't wait to hear what Scooter has to say about this," said Crystal.

# The blizzard

As Captain Ross picked up his radio to call base, a fierce wind blew up. Seconds later, the team was surrounded by a whirling, terrifying snowstorm.

"I've lost radio contact!" shouted the captain above the howling wind. "Keep close! Don't lose each other!"

The team huddled together in the stinging blast. The snow was so thick that they couldn't see one metre ahead.

"These blizzards can last for weeks!"
shouted Doc. "Head for the Cat!"
But it wasn't that easy...

It was impossible to move quickly in the blinding storm – or even to see the Caterpillar Outpost.

"We must find shelter soon!" Doc warned, after a few terrifying minutes.

"My people have lived with this weather for thousands of years!" called Crystal. "Everyone, kneel down!"

She showed the team how to use ice axes, knives and hands to dig a cave from the snow.

## Igloos

The snow houses built by the native people of the Arctic were not family homes. They were shelters that could be built quickly during hunting trips.

"Phew!" said Cosmo, crawling inside. "It's much warmer in here! But couldn't we have built a proper igloo?"

"In this weather?" laughed Crystal. "I'd like to see you try!"

Although the team members were warm and safe, they were still anxious.

"I wonder how Scooter is getting on?" said Crystal.

"He's probably worrying about us!" Doc said. "Don't you think, Cosmo?"

Cosmo did not answer. He was thinking about the meteorite outside.

While the team waited for the storm to end, Crystal told them about her people, the Inuit, and their way of life in the Arctic. She explained how they found food and made

*This wooden mask was worn by an Inuit shaman. The shaman acted as a link with the spirit world.*

clothes from animal skins. She described their art and spiritual beliefs.

Suddenly, the captain raised his hand. "Listen!" he said.

*Tradtionally, Inuit people were skilled craftworkers. They made beautiful carvings from bone or wood.*

The howling wind had stopped.

"It's over," said Doc. "Thanks to you, Crystal, we've survived."

"I'll radio Scooter and tell him we're safe," said the captain.

"Let's head for the Cat!" said Doc. "I need some supper!"

"I was afraid I'd have to start fishing through the ice," Crystal laughed.

"I'm not sure you would like raw fish!"

"Forget the fish!" grunted Cosmo. "Just let me take another look at that meteorite!"

"Not yet, Cosmo!" said Captain Ross. "Let's rest, eat and talk to Scooter first. If we rush, we may make mistakes."

Soon the hungry team was enjoying a hot meal in the Caterpillar Outpost.

"Food really matters at these low temperatures," said Doc. "Our bodies need energy to keep warm."

Just then, Crystal's sharp ears caught the faint sound of an engine.

"What a storm!" called Scooter,
as Doc flung open the door of the Cat.
"Am I glad to see you!"

"Believe me, we feel the same!"
replied Captain Ross. "Now you're here,
let's plan how we're going to examine
this meteorite..."

# The start of the adventure

Mission Meteorite was on track at last. It was time to show Scooter what Cosmo had found.

The team crunched through the powdery snow. No one was surprised when Cosmo hurried ahead.

"We'll find him nose to nose with a fossil," laughed Doc.

But seconds later, Cosmo came running back.

"I... don't... know... how to tell you," he panted. "The meteorite has split open and... it's empty!"

"What?" gasped Crystal.

"The creature inside–" Cosmo gulped. "It was alive!"

There was silence. Then Captain Ross took charge.

"I have a feeling," he said, "that this adventure is only just beginning..."

# Glossary

**Antarctic**
A region of snow and ice, at the most southern part of the Earth; the coldest place on Earth. Also see Arctic.

**Arctic**
A region of snow and ice, at the most northern part of the Earth. Also see Antarctic.

**Atmosphere**
A layer of gases around a planet.

**Crevasse**
A deep crack in the surface of an ice sheet.

**Extraterrestrial**
A creature from outer space.

**Fossils**
Fossils are the remains of dead animals or plants. The remains are preserved in rock, for thousands of years.

**Icebreaker**
A specially-strengthened ship. It is able to break through sheet ice blocking the seaway in front of it.

**Ice sheet**
A thick, permanent cover of ice.

**Inuit**
The native people who live in the Arctic region of Greenland and North America. There are about 25,000 Inuit in North America.

**Magnetic field**
The area around a magnet, where its effects can be felt.

**Meteor**
A tiny piece of dust or rock from space, which burns up as it enters Earth's atmosphere, leaving a streak of light. Meteors are sometimes called 'shooting stars'.

**Meteorite**
Some rocks from space are so big that they pass through Earth's atmosphere without completely burning up. They land and are then called meteorites.

**Northern Lights**
Glowing green, red or yellow lights that are seen in the sky near the North Pole. Similar lights, near the South Pole, are called the Southern Lights.

**Satellite**
A spacecraft which circles above the Earth, to collect information or carry out a certain job. For example, some satellites take pictures of Earth's surface. Others send television pictures around the world.

**Shaman**
A priest or medicine man.